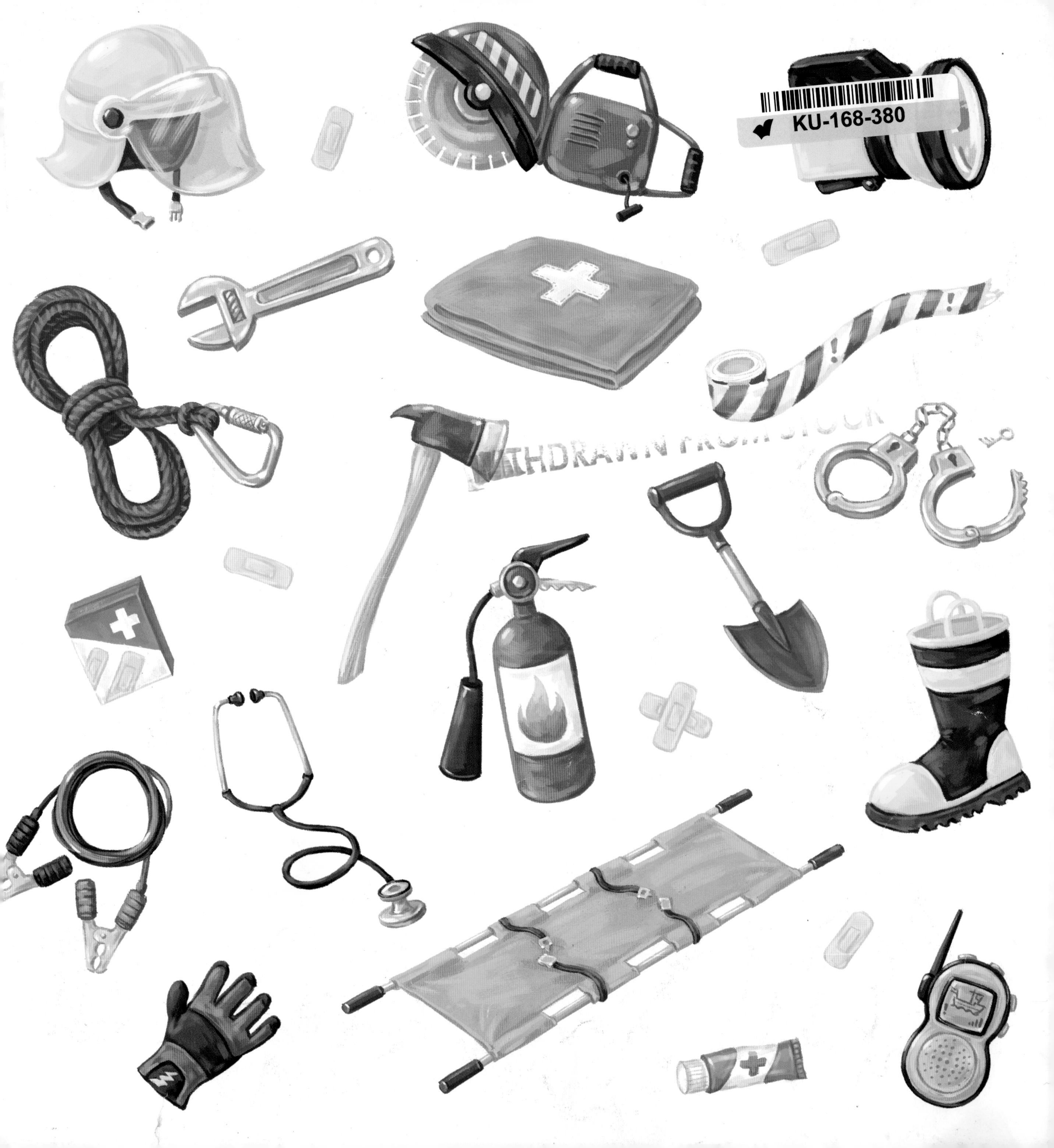

For Lila and Emma,
in loving memory of Ben Who Climbs Mountains xxx
S.P-H.

For Theodore xx
E.E.

READY, STEADY, RESCUE!

First published in Great Britain in 2017 by Hodder Children's Books

Hodder Children's Books
An imprint of Hachette Children's Group
Part of Hodder and Stoughton
Carmelite House, 50 Victoria Embankment
London EC4Y 0DZ

A catalogue record of this book is available from the British Library.

HB ISBN: 978 1 444 92925 6
PB ISBN: 978 1 444 92926 3
1 3 5 7 9 10 8 6 4 2
Printed in China

An Hachette UK Company
www.hachette.co.uk

Ready, Steady, RESCUE!

Smriti Prasadam-Halls & Ed Eaves

We're at **EMERGENCY CONTROL,**
To save and rescue is our goal.
Responding **FAST** to every call,
To every crisis, big or small.

For any rescue we're prepared.
We're very brave. We're never scared.
We'll always be there, come what may,
Ready, steady...

ON OUR WAY!

A **FIRE** at the baker's shop!
They need our help to make it stop!

FIRE TRUCK FLICK has got her hose.

Sound the siren! Off she goes!

Flames are **FIZZING**,

water **WHIZZING**,

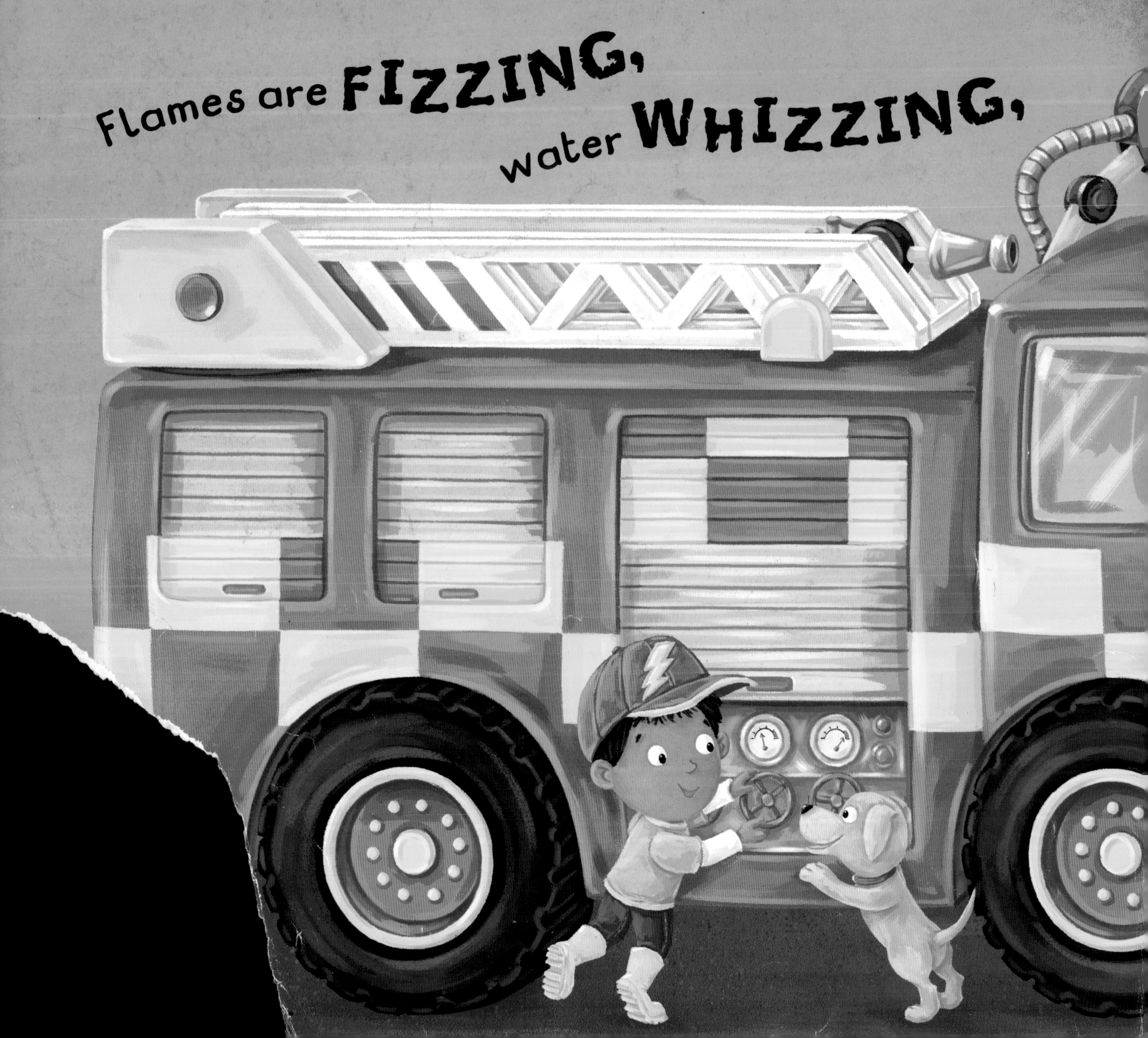

Fighting fire in a flash,
Ready, steady...
SPLASH,
SPLASH,
SPLASH!
SOS! A car's in trouble!
Help is wanted on the double!

TOW TRUCK TOM'S

the one they need.
Here he comes
to take the lead.

GRIPPING tight, with all his might,

Safely harnessed, nice and slow,
Ready, steady... ***TOW, TOW, TOW!***

MAYDAY! MAYDAY! Storm at sea!
Help is needed urgently!

LIFEBOAT LEELA launches fast,
Skims the water, speeding past.

Lightning **FLASHING,**

thunder **CRASHING,**

Leela's there to tow the boat,
Ready, steady...
FLOAT, FLOAT, FLOAT!
Robbers in a high-street store!
HELP! They're heading out the door!

Hurry, hurry, **POLICE CAR PETE,**
The thieves are zooming
down the street!

ROARING, RACING,

WHIZZING, CHASING,
Siren sings,
nee-nah, nee-nah,
Ready, steady...
STOP THAT CAR!
HELP is needed double quick!
The station master's very sick!

AMBULANCE AL has soothing gel,
And medicine to make her well.

DASHING, DARING, careful, caring,

Shut the doors and flash the light,
Ready, steady...
HOLD ON TIGHT!
DANGER on the snowy slope!
Climbers trapped without a rope!

HELICOPTER HARMIT'S here,
Blades a-whirring,
have no fear.

SEARCHING,
FINDING,
winch **UNWINDING,**

Strong and stable,
firm and swift,
Ready, steady... LIFT, LIFT, LIFT!

PHEW! It's time
to have a rest...
But what is this?
Who's in distress?
Danger, danger!
RED ALERT!
Big explosion, people hurt!

There's SO much work
we have to do...
We'll need the help
of **ALL THE CREW!**

Stop the traffic,
please make way,

Ready, steady...
SAVE THE DAY!

The smoke is thick. The work is tough,
But we are big and strong enough.
HEAVING,
STRETCHING,

PULLING,

FETCHING,

Help and rescue, lift and tow,

READY, STEADY...

GO,
GO,

GO!

What a busy day
it's been.
What a lot of things
we've seen.

Climbers rescued,
baddies caught,

Patients patched up,
fires fought.

Sturdy, steady, **EVER** ready,
Rescue team, we **SAVED** the day...

Rescue team,

HIP HIP

HOORAY!